LIFE'S SIMPLE PLEASURES

Sixth Avenue Books™ are published by:
AOL Time Warner Book Group
1271 Ave. of the Americas
New York, NY 10020

Visit our Web site at www.twbookmark.com

An AOL Time Warner Company

Printed in China
First printing: 10 9 8 7 6 5 4 3 2 1

ISBN: 1-931722-16-1

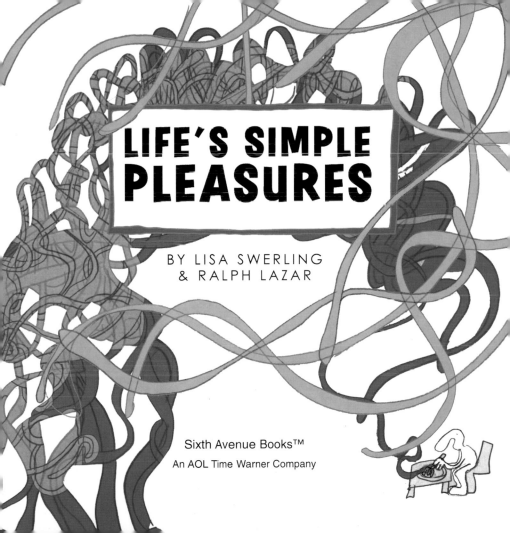

LIFE'S SIMPLE PLEASURES

BY LISA SWERLING
& RALPH LAZAR

Sixth Avenue Books™

An AOL Time Warner Company

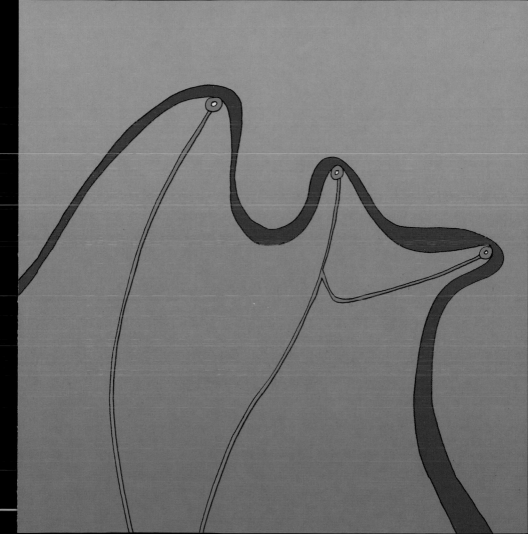

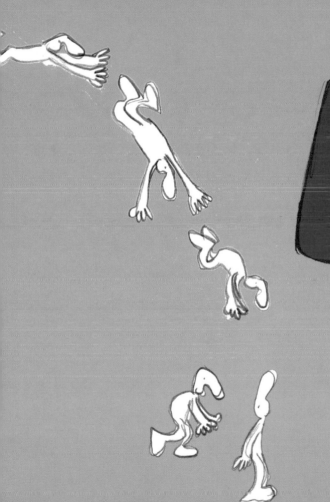

THERE'S NO SUCH THING AS TOO MUCH COFFEE

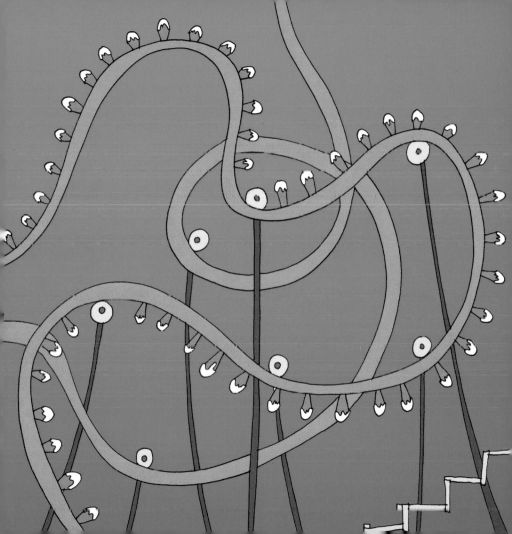

strawberry

pistachio

orange

Vanilla

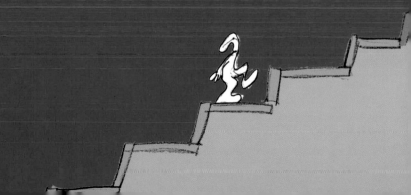

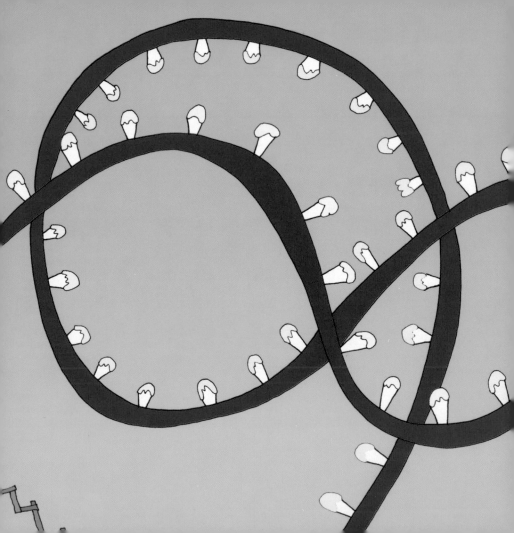

DANCING IS GOOD FOR YOUR HEALTH

...most of the time!

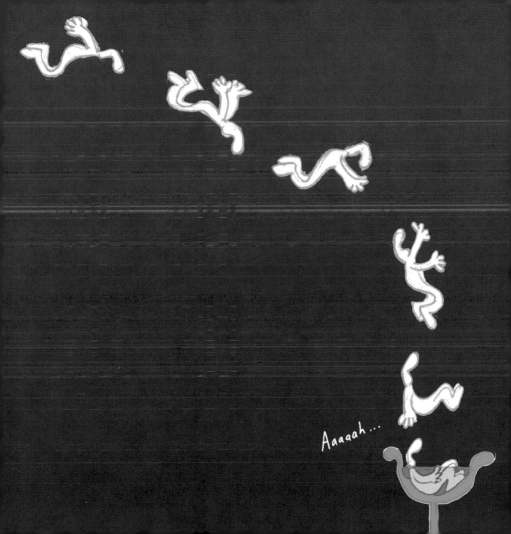

Aaaaah...

Brrrr-eathtaking....

PLAYING
IN THE
WAVES
KEEPS YOU
YOUNG

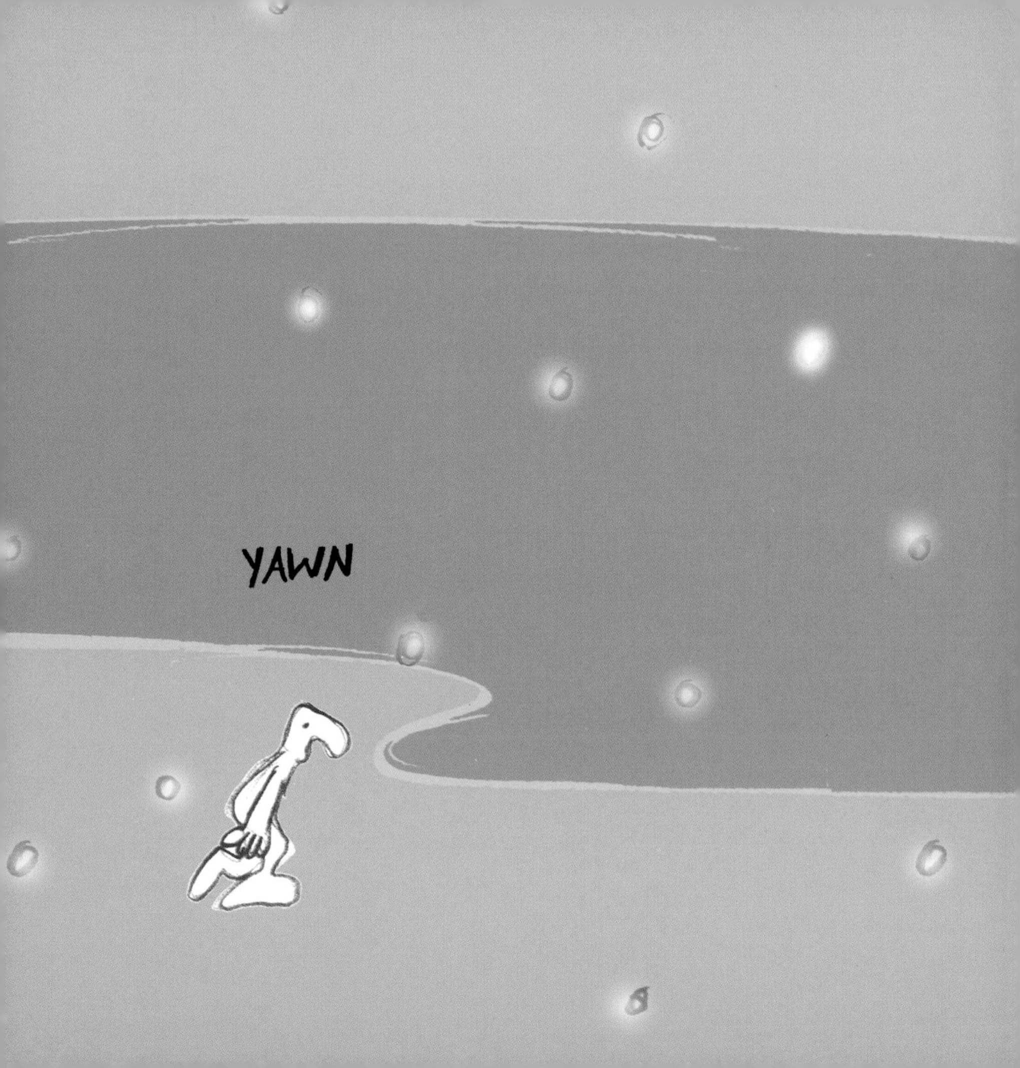
YAWN

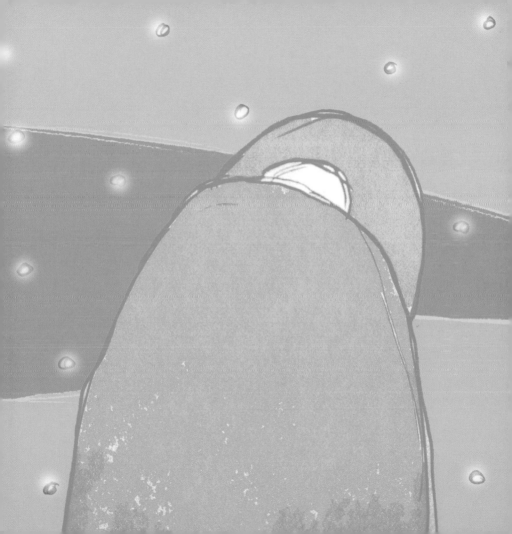

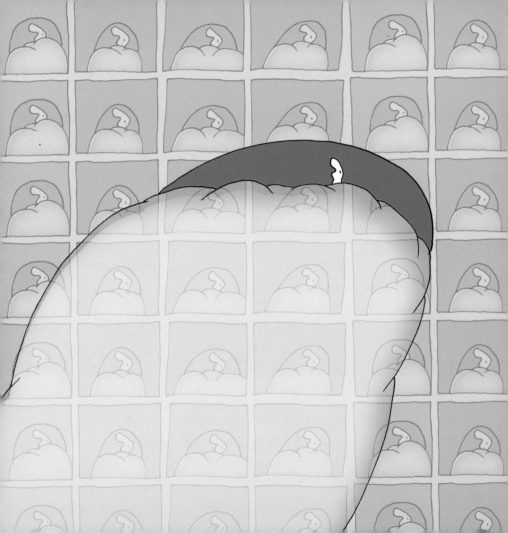

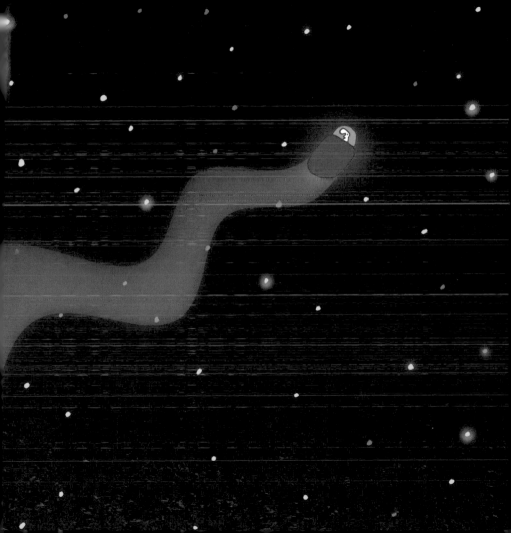

ABOUT THE AUTHORS

Ralph Lazar, Lisa Swerling and their daughter Bea are currently based in the UK. They have recently applied for visas to Harold's Planet, and are expected to move there as soon as the paperwork has been processed.

This book is for Barry, Jamie, Nicky and Hummagrecca